AF430408

Chapter 1: The beginning

I should have known better than to walk into an immortal bar. It's hard when you find the perfect woman only to find out you would leave them alone. Such is the sadness between human and immortal relationships.

I hope someday we can be together for eternity. For now, I'll be satisfied with a lifetime. Our relationship works, although I'll be a bit embarrassed to admit I didn't know she was famous.

You see, I had been at work studying books at the library and thought I deserved a nice drink. I was studying in Greece and navigating a place you aren't familiar with can be a challenge, especially when the only directions you can read are in Braille.

I can recognize a bar by sound though and when I heard the dance music and the sounds of laughter and people genuinely happy and enjoying themselves.

There were cheers when I entered the bar. I could hear a girl singing with the music and the cheers of appreciation from the crowd. "Atta girl Hebe! Sing your heart out!" As enjoyable as the music was, I tried to keep to a quieter area. I sat in a quiet area of the bar, and thought for a moment I was alone until I heard 'her' voice. Her tone was gruff at first. A woman's voice: "Do you have a death wish?"It startled me at first: "oh I'm sorry, I didn't realize someone was sitting here already."Woman: "Yeah, sure you didn't.""Oh no, I really didn't. I can't see you."Woman:"what are you, blind?""Why yes, actually I am."

She paused and then sighed: "Life can be cruel at times."

"Life can be wonderful too. All you need do is believe in yourself."

She grumps: "People are afraid of me. As well they should be! I can kill them all!"

"Why would you want to go and do a thing like that?"

"Because it's what I do! I have snakes for hair, I'm hideous! People who look at me get turned to stone! Do you understand? Do you know who I am?!"

"That sounds amazing actually. No, we haven't formally been introduced. I'm Harmony. It's a pleasure to meet you." I held a hand out to her, or at least in the direction of her voice. She didn't take my hand.

"I'm Medusa. Why aren't you afraid of me?"

"I've learned not to judge people by what others say. Since I can't see, I judge people by their actions and their hearts rather than how people look. It's actually rather convenient not to be able to see. This way I can't judge someone on their looks."

Medusa scowled: "How can you judge anything at all?   You have no frame of reference! You can't see so you don't know what people think. People say more with their actions and it's harder to pretend."

H: "I don't have your frame of reference but I have my own. You can tell in someone's voice, in someone's touch, how they really feel."

Harmony's hand softly touched Medusa's cheek. Her touch was gentle like a butterfly's kiss. It startled Medusa and she jerked back.

Harmony lowered her hand: "My apologies. I didn't mean to startle you. Without sight, my hands act as my eyes. It's a very different experience I've been told."

Medusa stuttered: "A..aren't you scared of me? Scared my snakes might bite you? That you might get poisoned?"

Harmony smiled brightly: "Why should I be? If they bite me, it will have been my fault for startling them. Besides, it feels more like you are the one afraid. I don't know you, but I'd like to get to know you if you'll let me."

Medusa settled a bit and looked around. The music had died down and many were staring at her. Harmony didn't seem to notice one bit. Her focus was on Medusa and Medusa alone.

Medusa grabbed Harmony's hand and glaring at any in her way, dragged Harmony from the bar, and down several unfamiliar paths that they seemed to fight through the wind through. Medusa didn't say a word until they stopped.

Medusa had her sit on a stone bench: This is a special spot for me.....

Harmony: "I smell fresh flowers and I can hear birds chirping. Where are we?"

Medusa:"My private garden. It's more peaceful than that awful bar."

Harmony: "it sounds beautiful."

"It is. Especially in the spring and summer"

Harmony: "Do you want to talk?"

Medusa: "What would I want to talk about?"

Harmony: "Whatever you want to talk about. You brought us here."

Medusa began pacing, her snakes hissing in agitation. "I don't know why I brought you out here. You couldn't possibly understand my situation."

Harmony: "I may not understand but I'm a good listener and I'm happy to be a friendly ear."

Medusa: "I don't understand you. How can you be so calm? Do you not understand who I am? What I'm capable of? I could kill you! I could turn you to stone!"

Harmony: "I know who you said you are, and I've heard the stories of someone bearing your name with snakes for hair who turns people to stone, but I am also of the belief that there are always at least two sides to every story. I would love to get to know who you are as a person rather than the stories people tell about you."

Medusa: "I....I'm not sure I want to tell you. Or who I really am anymore."

Harmony: "We can be friends. I'm sure there's lots you can teach me. I'm not sure what I can teach you in return but I'd be happy to try. If nothing else, I can be a friendly ear. I'm not going to gossip and spread rumors. I think you have enough of those going around."

Medusa: "How.....how can we possibly be friends? You'll be ostracized by the gods if you befriend me."

Harmony: "I'm not afraid. Besides, if they wanted to be friends, they would take the first step and approach me. If they approach me with ulterior motives, I like to think I'll be able to tell. But something drew me to you in the bar. And I'd like to get to know you. Are you willing to be friends?"

Medusa: "I.....guess I have nothing to lose....."

Chapter 2: Time marches on

The bond between us began to grow. Medusa and I started spending time together a couple times a week. Sometimes it was time in the garden, and sometimes it was just a bite to eat. Let me tell you, Medusa is a phenomenal cook. I keep telling her she should become a professional chef but she keeps denying the suggestion stating that no one would accept a chef that turns people to stone   Months went by and we grew closer. The time we spent together increased and our time was comfortable.

One day, as we enjoyed some sweet wine and a warm fire, I pushed Medusa a bit. I wanted to see her with my own hands. I wanted to know her face rather than imagining the depiction her stories portrayed because I knew she was so much more than those harsh tales that kept her as a villain, a monster.

Harmony settled closer to Medusa in the warmth of the fireplace. "You know, you haven't let me see you yet."Medusa laughed: "That's a bad joke. Besides, you wouldn't want to see me if you could."Harmony snuggled and put her head on Medusa's shoulder: "It's not a joke. I told you before, my hands are my eyes. I can see better with my hands than many see with their eyes. I'm not afraid. I know enough about you to know what you are really like. I know you, how you really are. I enjoy our time together, but it feels incomplete without knowing your face."Medusa sighed heavily like it was a chore to agree to let Harmony touch her face: "If it means that much to you, then I guess......I'll trust you enough to let you know my face. But don't blame me if my snakes bite! I've warned you they are quite temperamental."Harmony: "I'll be careful. I promise."Medusa nodded slowly and took Harmony's hand in hers, slowly bringing it to her cheek. Harmony slowly brought her other hand to Medusa's other cheek and ran her fingers over every line and muscle like a sculptor preparing her finest work. Then moved her hands over Medusa's hair, gently caressing the snakes. Medusa prepared herself for the reaction everyone else gave her. The scream and run like their lives depended on it. Harmony was slow though and meticulous. When she finished, she sat back in silence for a moment then slowly she let out a breath. Medusa winced, putting her defenses back up so she wouldn't get hurt. Harmony's next word was so quiet, Medusa had to ask her to repeat it.
"Beautiful."Medusa's confusion was evident: "What?"Harmony: "You are beautiful. I had no idea how stunning you are."Medusa: "I....I haven't had someone tell me that in a very very long time."Harmony: "The people around you lately are blinded by their own desires if they can't see how beautiful you are, inside and out. Medusa, you have the light in you like a star hidden behind the sun and not allowed to shine, but let me tell you something. I may be blind, but I can see your beauty and your spirit."Tears welled in Medusa's eyes: "Harmony, why do you have to be this way?"Harmony: "What way?" She wiped a tear awayMedusa: "You make me want to be human again."

Harmony held her close: "You are human. You never stopped being human. You just got a few extra abilities out of the deal."

Medusa laughed: "Just a few deadly ones. I....I never told you what happened, did I?"

Harmony: "You mean how you got your curse? No, you haven't, and you don't have to if you don't want to. It's not that I don't want to know the real story, but I know it's caused you a lot of pain over the years and I don't want to ever cause you any pain."

Medusa: "I don't think you would harm any living creature if you could help it. I think I.... I feel like I can trust you with my story. My truth. Let me take you back first. To the world I lived in...."

Images began popping into Harmony's mind as Medusa spoke, the huge columns of the temples and the mountains. The next image presented to her was that of a young woman, beautiful and full of life. She had only natural beauty, none of the trappings of makeup to give her a false look. She walked by a large man who was eyeing her. She was on her way to temple and thought only of her goal.

The man tried to get her attention, to flirt and impress, but she kindly averted his favors and insisted she needed to get to temple. Enraged, the man followed her into the temple. He grabbed at the young woman and made her no longer pure.

The goddess of the temple, enraged by the act, arrived. The goddess by nature, is stunning in figure but one should never anger a goddess.

The man revealed himself to be a god. The goddess, having no recourse to punish the god, chose to punish the girl instead.

Goddess: "For the crime of defiling my temple, I sentence you to an eternity of resentment and loneliness."

The beautiful girl changed. Her olive skin became green and scaly. Her beautiful brunette locks became living snakes.

Goddess: "Be forewarned, your looks are now frightful and any who gaze upon you and you gaze back at them will be turned to stone, unable to share their frightful tale. Now be gone from my sight."

The images faded with the last images of the god smirking and of the girl running from the temple.

As Medusa finished her tale, all Harmony could do was cry for her friend. Cry for the cruel injustice. "How could they do that to you? You had done nothing wrong."

Medusa: "Fate can be a cruel mistress. My life has extended. I would be long dead if it hadn't happened. I...it's hard sometimes to live for eternity alone."

Harmony: "You should not have had to suffer such a fate. It was the God at fault, not you."

Medusa: "Athena could not punish her uncle and therefore punished me instead. I was the one she could vent her anger on without causing herself problems. The relationship between Poseidon and Athena was already strained at that point because of their competition over Athens. When Athena won, Poseidon did not take it well."

Harmony: "You were the victim on both accounts. That isn't right." She paused a moment sniffling as a thought hit her. "Speaking of victims...wasn't there a legend that a demigod killed you?"

Medusa: "Yes, I remember that story. He killed a Gorgon but it wasn't me. My form was bestowed upon me as a curse, but some beings were born this way. Most of the myths about me aren't actually mine. People assumed that it was me so I started laying low. Most people thought I died so the mortals started leaving me alone. I was able to find a place where I could settle down. With makeup, I could almost pass for a human long enough to get essentials."

Harmony: "You never need to hide from me. I may not have sight but I see you as you are."

Medusa hugged Harmony close and settled with her. A week later, Medusa wanted to take Harmony to a concert.

Chapter 3: A night out

M: "This is the Odeon of Herodes Atticus. It is an open air theatre and has many grand performances here, both musical and theatrical. Imagine grand arches 3 stories high and the seating holds well over 4,000 people. I have been coming here for centuries. Even if you can't see it, you can enjoy the music. The performer tonight is an orchestra. I hope you enjoy it." Medusa had settled with Harmony away from much of the crowd but not so far that the music was faint. She gave Harmony's hand a small squeeze and settled in to watch the performance. She enjoyed the peace between them.

The evening was nice. The music filled the cool air with a feeling of joy. They waited till the very end to leave so the mortals wouldn't notice Medusa. As they finally descended the lengthy steps, the darkness grew peaceful. The stars above shone like diamonds in the sky. Medusa thought it was perfect....until some hooligans at the bottom started haggling some poor tourist. Harmony didn't know exactly what was going on but could hear the tourist pleading for her things and the hooligans laughing. Harmony took her walking stick and hit one of them hard: "Leave her alone!"

One of the three guys grabbed onto Harmony's arm roughly and Medusa was mad: "Let her go before you wish for eternity that you had never laid eyes on me."

Medusa's head was still covered by a cloak but her snakes began hissing in anger. The guy laughed: "And just what do you think you're going to do about it?"

Medusa raised her head and stared him straight in the eyes and then.....he stared back. Medusa stared for a long moment then blinked: "What?"

The guys laughed: "Was something supposed to happen? Were you expecting some knight in shining armor?"

The second guy: "Or maybe a handsome prince?"

The third guy: "Nah, maybe she just thought that God would smite me."

The three guys laughed then the second one went to grab Medusa: "That's okay freak, I'll be your handsome prince."

The guys all started to laugh until Harmony whacked the first guy holding her, then the second guy: "Don't talk about her like that! She is worth more than any of you bumbling idiots! Or should I say cackling hyenas? No, that would be an insult to the creatures."

The first guy: "Why you little...!" He went for Harmony. Medusa grabbed Harmony's hand and told her to run. The tourist took advantage and grabbed her stuff and ran the opposite direction.

Medusa tried her best to keep Harmony from falling, but she stumbled a lot in the darkness. Harmony: "I wasn't made for running!"

Medusa: "We don't have much choice right now. This way."

They went down several side streets before stopping, panting hard. Harmony: "W...why d...did we have to...to run?"

Medusa: "I couldn't turn them to stone. I tried and he looked right into my eyes but....but..."

Harmony: "Let's get back to your place. We can talk there. It will be okay."

Medusa nodded and took Harmony home. She got them some cocoa and marshmallows and settled in front of the fire.

Harmony: "Has that ever happened? Where you couldn't turn someone to stone? I mean I'm not saying you should go around doing that but...you seemed really upset by it."

Medusa shook her head: "No, never. I mean it has always been that if I look at someone and they look back at me that they turn to stone. That's it. Game over. My finishing move, they never bother me again. This time though....I couldn't. I tried. I focused. My one superpower that came out of this curse! And now.....it's gone."

Harmony hugged her: "It's okay. Maybe it was a fluke? Or maybe the curse was lifted a little?"

Medusa: "why would anyone lift the curse on me? I'm the villain they love to hate. I'm mean and scary and people love to hate."

Harmony: "People get scared easily. They question the unknown and get scared if they don't understand it. You shouldn't be hated. You did nothing wrong. You are special and unique. You are a treasure. You have a golden heart and it comes out in your actions. You care."

Medusa:"I care too much. I'm immortal. What do you think is going to happen? We can't live happily ever after. This isn't some fairytale! You are mortal. You will die, and I will be left alone again. I can't care about you, or anyone."

Harmony: "Medusa, I know this has you spooked, but I promise it will be okay. Trust me."

Medusa: "I think it's best you not be around me. It was foolish of me to think that I could be anything but cursed. When I start to relax, people get hurt. I...I don't want to see you again. I'll take you home but then we're done. I don't know you, you don't know me. Clear?"

Harmony: "No, not clear. Can't you tell that I want to be with you? I want to be your friend."

Medusa's snakes hiss: "don't you get it? I'm a monster! You will never change that! I am who I am! Let me be before I....before I turn you to stone!"

Medusa ran off upset. Harmony tried to pursue her but couldn't follow the sound of her steps falling for long.

Saddened, Harmony returned home. She gave Medusa a couple days to try to settle then went searching for her. She tried all the places they had been together; her garden, her home, even the bar. She asked around to check if anyone knew where Medusa was, but people can be cruel and some didn't know, and many didn't care. Those that didn't care made snide remarks both about Medusa and the girl who searched in vain for her lost friend; a friendship she cherished greatly.

Weeks went by, then months with no sign nor sound from Medusa. Just as Harmony was losing hope, she made a new friend at a local cafe. She was enjoying an espresso and staying warm from the cold air when someone sat down in the chair in front of her.

Chapter 4: Hope

A woman's soft voice greeted her: "Why so blue, my friend?"

Harmony: "Lost hope. How could you tell?"

The woman gently touched Harmony's hands: "I have a gift for it. Care to share your tale of woe? I can listen and you may feel better."

Harmony: "Thank you for your kind offer, but I'm afraid I don't even know your name."

The woman chuckled: "Please forgive my manners. My name is Cyrene and you are?"

"I'm Harmony. It's nice to meet you. But pray tell, why would you want to hear my story?"

"I am a story keeper of sorts. I like to find them happy endings."

Harmony: "That's very thoughtful of you but I'm not sure you can help me. I'm looking for a dear friend who does not wish to be found. She has scars that run deep and I wasn't able to help her overcome them."

Cyrene leaned in close: "People are all afraid of something. It's a matter of finding the courage to see past it. Often, people can't do it alone. They need someone as a catalyst to bind their courage to them. Why do you think great hero's usually have a sidekick to support them?"

Harmony laughed. The sound was almost foreign to her since Medusa left: "Yes, I suppose you're right. It's....it's worth a try anyway, right?"

Cyrene grinned: "Yep. Worth a try."

Harmony slowly divulged her troubled story: "My friend is unique. She has snakes for hair and she usually wears a cloak to cover herself. She was hurt badly and there was an incident with some hooligans. They were attacking an innocent tourist and my friend protected us. She was so upset by the incident that she ran off and I haven't seen her since. I don't think she's even been home in that time and I'm worried about her. What if something happened to her?"

Cyrene: "I'm sure she will be fine. You need to trust in her abilities. How long has it been?"

Harmony: "Several months now."

Cyrene: "Have you checked Poros? It has some forests that would make it a great place to hide. It's only an hour or two away by ferry from Athens main port, Piraeus. If I was going to run off, it would probably be to go there. It's late today but if you want to go tomorrow, I'll take you."

Harmony: "I never thought of checking the nearby islands. I kept staying to the mainland. That's a great idea. What time would you like to meet tomorrow so we can go?"

Cyrene arranges for them to meet about 8 in the morning so they can board the ferry at Piraeus by 10. Harmony was so excited, she showed up an hour early. She sipped at her coffee and studied a book she purchased about the local geography and culture. It was a hard book to find in Braille.

Cyrene made a rather loud arrival, making Harmony jump. Cyrene: "Well hi there! Somebody's an early riser. Didn't we say 8? I'm pretty sure we said 8, right?"

Harmony: "Oh, yes. I just couldn't sleep so I came early. It's not 8 yet is it? I don't recall my alarm going off on my phone."

Cyrene: "No, no, I came early too, just not nearly so. You've been here a while, haven't you little miss?"

Harmony blushed: "Ah, yes, I came about 7ish. Do you want something to eat or drink?"

Cyrene: "I'll take a coffee to go. We can walk to the port. It's a nice day and we're only a little early. Plenty of time to walk. Even if we didn't make the first boat, we could catch the next one."

Harmony: "I'll order you a coffee then. It's on me for helping me."

Cyrene: "If you say so. I'm not mandating it. But there you'll have to pay for Meadow."

Harmony: "You mean Medusa?"

Cyrene: "Yeah, her. Your girlfriend."

Harmony blushed: "she's not my girlfriend. We're just friends."

Cyrene: "Yeah, sure, I believe that like I believe there's spring in the underworld. And no, just because Persephone spent time in the underworld does not mean that she brought spring there."

Harmony: "What...? You believe the old legends?"

Cyrene: "Of course. There is more to this world than you know. You just need to open your eyes to see it."

Harmony: "I'm blind."

Cyrene laughs: "Blind? You see through the illusions of people straight to their heart. I haven't met a mortal that could see so well in centuries."

Harmony was startled: "C.....centuries?"

Cyrene giggled: "Oh, am I showing my age? Never mind that. I'll help you find Medusa. Just remember to keep looking at people with eyes that see through illusion to the heart. It's an important trait."

Harmony: "Ah, y...yes."

Cyrene: "Let's go then. We don't want to be late."

Harmony: "Late? Do you mean we're expected?"

Cyrene: "Ah no, I actually need to do someone a favor while we're there. Don't worry, nothing serious."

Harmony: "It's a relief actually. That you are going there for more than just me. I was trying to think of how I could thank you for your help."

Cyrene: "Help comes back around when you need it. You just needed a little guiding. Most young ones do. In some way or another."

Harmony: "I'm not exactly a young child."

Cyrene: "Youth, like beauty, is in the eye of the beholder. Haven't you ever heard the saying that you are as young as you feel?"

Harmony: "Ah, yes, I've heard that saying before but I'm not sure it applies to youth in the literal sense."

Cyrene: "You see through illusions well, but your eyes are still not fully open. Perhaps we will fix that at some point. For now, let's get our drinks and go. It's a beautiful day for a walk."

Harmony quickly ordered a couple coffees to go and followed closely behind with her things.

Cyrene: "While we walk, so you want to know more about Athens?"

Harmony perked up: "Oh yes! I love learning about different places. Sometimes people can describe them so well that I can almost picture it."

Cyrene: "Ah, yes, and take you back in time as well I'm sure."

Harmony chuckled: "Yes, of course."

Cyrene: "Did you know they built a long wall along Athens? It was a long long time ago and little of it remains today. They started building it back in 493 BC at the Port of Piraeus. The very port we are going to. It was designed to help protect Athens and the port provided housing for many ships. The wall provided protection from multiple attacks from Sparta. The port actually housed 3 locations from which ships could disembark. One for pedestrian use, and the other two for military. Athens was named for the Goddess Athena but there are actually multiple Gods represented here. There is a temple dedicated to the God of the Forge. It was well built and well preserved. I would expect nothing less from a temple dedicated to Hephaestus. It actually used to house metalwork shops. Hephaestus and his hammer, he does fine work. Naturally the king of the gods also has a temple here. The Temple of the Olympian Zeus is actually the largest temple ever made."

Harmony: "I think I heard about that temple. Didn't it take a long time to build?"

Cyrene: "Indeed. Longer than you've been alive, or even a mortal lifetime in this century. It took 700 years to build. Imagine 104 columns 17 metres high and inside it, a massive statue of Zeus himself! Large enough sitting that if the statue were to stand, it would be so large as to blow the roof off his own temple!"

Harmony: "Oh my! I imagine that would be quite large and impressive."

Cyrene: "Fitting for the king of the Gods, isn't it? Oh but there's one more place I want to tell you about. As I am sure you are familiar with Medusa's story, how she came to be?"

Harmony saddened at the mention: "It was not a just punishment. Medusa was innocent."

Cyrene: "Of course she was, but Athena is not a dummy. She is a goddess of wisdom for a reason. While she and Poseidon have had their bouts, sometimes it is wiser not to start a war. Believe it or not, Poseidon has a temple here. It's called the Temple of Sounion. The temple was the last view of Athenian land for warriors and seafarers leaving home. This may have been a city claimed by Athena, but Poseidon had just as large an impact on the people here. Do you see now why Athena didn't try to punish Poseidon? Yes, he had acted in a way unbefitting a God, but she could not sink to her uncle's level. She made the wisest decision at the time, and that was not to punish her uncle. Do you know that her actions were actually a gift to Medusa?"

Harmony was horrified: "A gift? She took everything from Medusa. Medusa was fearful of even going home to her family after that. How could she possibly have viewed the curse as a gift?"

Cyrene was amused: "You are used to looking at things differently, aren't you? Do you think that your views of the world would have been the same if you had the same sight as Medusa? You would have run in fear of Medusa if you had met her and saw her as everyone else does. Instead, because you were cursed without physical sight, you don't have any of those superficial images."

Harmony: "I....I never thought of it that way. I accepted my world was darker than others, but just in a way that was different. I never viewed it as a curse."

Cyrene: "Nor should you, my dear. Because your lack of physical sight has helped to preserve your good heart and pure nature. Hold onto that as long as you can, because once you lose it, you can't get it back. When we get to the island, there is someone I want you to meet."

Cyrene continued to tell her about Athens on the way to the ferry and let it be peaceful silence between them on the ferry trip. Peace and tranquility, a perfect time for reflection, Cyrene had called it.

Cyrene: "Welcome to the island of Poros. It's an island filled with natural beauty. Watch your step as we embark on this new place for you. Each time you find somewhere new, it is not the end of an adventure, merely the beginning of a new chapter. I spent several years on this island. I don't spend a lot of time here anymore, so I lend the place to a friend. That is the someone I want you to meet." Cyrene dragged Harmony off to a home that was rather secluded but the instant they got close, it smelled of fresh flowers and flowering trees. It was a place of spring in the middle of winter.

Harmony: "What is this place?"

Cyrene: "It's a place that make me feel like home."

A young woman's voice cut across the peace: "Who are you and what are you doing here? I warn you, I am Persephone, Goddess of the Underworld and I..."

Cyrene: "Now cut that out and be nice to our guest! This lovely lady is Harmony."

Harmony: "Did she say Goddess of the Underworld? Wasn't Persephone only in the underworld for 3 months out of the year?"

Cyrene: "Yes, that was before she went and got married. It was a lovely ceremony but this is not Persephone. Persephone would have more manners."

The young woman snorted:"I have plenty of manners!"

Cyrene: "Disrespectful ones if you ask me."

The young woman stomped her feet: "I didn't ask you! In fact, no one asked you!" Harmony felt sudden warmth from the young woman whose temper it seemed had ignited, literally.

Cyrene: "Darling, you have your father's temper."

The blue flames receded as she regained composure: "Cyrene, you are a despicable nymph."

Cyrene: "Why thank you dear. That's quite the compliment from the Nightmare Queen."

Harmony: "Nightmare Queen?"

Cyrene: "Indeed. Melinoe here is actually Persephone's daughter, but also Hades' daughter. Her job is nightmares and she is rather good at it, if a bit young."

Harmony: "I had no idea they had a child."

Melinoe: "Most people are scared of me, because I'm a nightmare."

Cyrene: "Now, now, that's your job sweetie, and your mom worries about how much you get into your work."

Melinoe: "Why are you here with her?"

Cyrene: "Because she is here searching for Medusa and I thought it would be good for her to meet someone strong like you who isn't her work."

Melinoe: "Oh, well, okay... I....I guess I can forgive the intrusion then. Come in. I have cookies. Fresh baked with cinnamon."

Harmony: "That sounds delightful, thank you."

Harmony and Cyrene follow Melinoe inside a quaint cottage. Inside smelled of fresh baked cookies cinnamon and raisin. There was a sense of peace and warmth in the cottage.

Cyrene: "Melinoe, why don't you tell Harmony about yourself?"

Melinoe: "Oh, I um, what would I say?"

Cyrene: "Well, you could tell her about why you live here instead of in the underworld."

Melinoe: "There is no peace in the underworld. If I am going to have a job where I am swimming in nightmares, I will have some peace and tranquility in my life."

Cyrene: "See Harmony? It's all about balance. You just need to find your balance with Medusa. Melinoe, is Medusa at her cottage?"

Melinoe: "Of course she is. She's in hiding again. What scared her this time?"

Cyrene: "Perhaps this time, it was commitment."

Melinoe: "Not likely. Do you want me to drop her a line?"

Cyrene: "Please. That would make things so much simpler than trying to track her down."

Melinoe disappeared into another room to make a call.

Harmony: "So Miss Melinoe knows Medusa?"

Cyrene: "Of course she does. She's used Medusa's negative image in human nightmares. And sometimes helps her by frightening those that Medusa doesn't want near her but doesn't want to turn to stone. She's not a bad person, but you knew that already."

Harmony: "I'm glad she has friends she can rely on. Even if she ran from me."

Cyrene: "Try not to be too upset about that. She was a bit freaked out."

Harmony: "I don't fully understand why she was so 'freaked out' as you put it."

Cyrene: "As I understand it, she lost her way to protect herself. That can be scary at first. Especially if you rely heavily on it. And believe me, she relies heavily on having her stone gaze as a trump card."

Harmony: "I understand. I wish she could have relied on me instead."

Cyrene: "People take time to change. Especially those who have lived as long as she has. Don't worry, she will be here soon. Have a cookie." Cyrene hands her an apple cinnamon cookie and nibbles on one herself.

Harmony nibbles at the cookie lost in thought.

Melinoe returned to the room: "Alright, she is begrudgingly coming over. She's waiting till dark so we have time."

Cyrene: "Oh good. How about a nice outdoor dinner with fireflies and and crystals?"

Melinoe: "Don't harm any of my plants. But you may setup a romantic dinner for them."

Harmony: "Ah, romantic dinner?"

Cyrene: "Of course. You want to sweep Medusa off her feet right? We'll help you do it."

Harmony's face practically glowed it was so red from her blush: "I, we're just friends!"

Cyrene and Melinoe both stared at Harmony like they didn't believe a word she said. Harmony couldn't see the looks but she could feel it.

Harmony: "I, we, um...."

Cyrene: "Medusa hasn't shown interest in anyone like that in all the time we've known her. By the way, your face is so red, it would shame the red-red rose."

Harmony: "Ah..."

Melinoe: "A simple thank you will suffice. Cyrene, I'll get her dressed and her hair done. You get the garden ready but I swear, if you hurt my plants, I will hurt you."

Cyrene chuckled: "Understood."

Melinoe took Harmony into her room and sat her down in front of a vanity facing away from the mirror: "Let's see.... we don't want you fading into the foliage, so green is out, oh, I have a stunning blue dress that would flatter your figure, with some gold accents, it will be perfect. Naturally we will need to do your hair in an updo. Maybe a bun with some curls coming down the sides to give you a little umph. It with look great with the dress, I hope you don't mind a low back. It will look stunning. Just put your faith in me and I'll make you look perfect. Medusa won't be able to tear her eyes from you."

Harmony: "I appreciate what you are trying to do but is this really um, necessary?"

Melinoe paused a moment: "IIoney, when you are trying to catch your lover's attention, no detail is too small. Now, let's get your makeup done. A nice soft pink for the lips and we will play up your pretty blue eyes with a smokey eye makeup."

Harmony: "I um, I'm in your hands."

Melinoe: "That's the spirit!"

Chapter 5: Magic night

That night, Medusa came cloaked in darkness to Mclinoc's homc. As she got close, there were quartz crystals glowing with iridescent shimmers lighting her path to the garden. Confused, she followed the path. More crystals decorated the garden, with one forming a stunning table in the middle of the garden. Fireflies danced around the edges of the garden making the place look like a fairy's garden. At the table sat a cloaked figure. Medusa assumed it was Melinoe and sat down at the crystal table with her. She removed her cloak and her snakes hissed in response to Medusa's anxiousness. She hated relying on others for help but when Melinoe offered assistance, she accepted. She worried that the curse would get worse before it got better.

Medusa: "I'm here. So tell me, how can you help?"

Harmony's voice came from the cloaked figure: "I will help however I can. I'll be there for you when you are stressed and don't know where to turn." She slowly removed the hood of the cloak: "I hope this wasn't too much for you. Melinoe and Cyrene insisted it was necessary."

Medusa was startled and in awe: "You...you look beautiful. I...."

Harmony: "Looks aren't everything. Appearances don't mean anything to me because I can't see it and I don't feel the necessity for it. But I want to be here for you if you will let me."

Medusa: "I...I may have overreacted.... I was just worried about getting into another situation like that. I mean, I couldn't protect you. We ended up having to run. My curse hasn't changed in a long time. What if it gets worse?"

Harmony took Medusa's hands in her own: "Then we will face it together."

Harmony stood and embraced Medusa: "I was worried about you."

Medusa hugged back: "I know. I'm sorry. I got scared.... it's not so easy to change old habits."

Harmony: "Please rely on me in the future."

Medusa: "I will try."

Cyrene: "Great, now that that's over, it's time to eat." Dishes began floating to the table.

Harmony: "They prepares a scrumptious feast for us. They're very kind."

Medusa: "They are suspicious but I guess kind is one way to put it. Alright, let's eat and then I'll take you home."

Cyrene: "The ferry isn't running anymore tonight. You'll have to wait to go back until morning."

Medusa: "Speak for yourself. Harmony can stay at my place here. You can figure out your own way home."

Cyrene: "I'll stay with Melinoe tonight."

Cyrene left them to chat amongst themselves, then Medusa took Harmony to her cottage on the island. It wasn't as big as her place on the mainland, but it afforded shelter and privacy.

Harmony and Medusa spent the next day traveling the islands before returning to the mainland. Medusa enjoyed describing the world she saw and delighted in Harmony's enthusiastic responses.

Months passed and they soon put the event behind them and again grew close. Without the concern of turning people to stone, they could spend more time out and about. Medusa still needed to keep her head covered but she found ways to enjoy time with Harmony in public.

Chapter 6: A special gift

An event soon came up, a Halloween party that Persephone and Hades we're hosting. Melinoe decided to invite the two and advised it was a masquerade ball so they should wear masks. Medusa was startled to receive the invitation but Harmony was so excited, Medusa couldn't very well turn it down. She took advantage of the coming event to spoil Harmony. They had a total girls day. They went shopping, got their nails done. Then Medusa did Harmony's hair up for her and did her makeup. Medusa has helped pick out Harmony's dress. It was a deep green which accented her hair and eyes. She then went darker on the lips and light on her eye makeup since she would be wearing a mask. Medusa was having more fun dressing Harmony up than doing her own makeup.

Medusa: "I wish you could see how beautiful you are."

Harmony: "I don't need to. Appearances never meant anything to me. You know that."

Medusa: "I know, but I wish just once you could share the fun and see yourself the way I see you."

Harmony: "You know, I wish the same thing. I wish you could see how wonderful you are. And I don't need to see you to know it."

Cyrene: "You know, I can help you with that."

Medusa: "Where did you come from? Don't enter peoples homes without permission!"

Cyrene chuckled: "Where would be the fun in telling you when I was going to pay you a visit? You might decide not to be home if you're feeling particularly lonely."

Harmony: "That doesn't make sense. Why would she leave if she's lonely and expecting you?"

Cyrene: "Because sometimes people don't want to be around people even though they're lonely. That's usually when they need someone like me to pop in."

Medusa: "Feel free not to pop in on me any more."

Cyrene: "Come now, you know you love it."

Medusa: "No, I really don't. But let's go back to what you said. You can really let Harmony see? You're not just messing with us?"

Cyrene: "Absolutely. I can. If that's really what you both want."

Harmony: "That would be amazing but it might be a bit too much to ask."

Medusa: "Not for me. Cyrene, give her sight." She cleared her throat: "Please."

Cyrene: "Okay. Sure. But there's something I need to make it happen."

Medusa: "What do you need?"

Cyrene: "In order to give her sight, I need sight to give. Temporarily of course. Here's the deal. You, Medusa,would need to agree to give up your sight until Midnight. In exchange, I will give Harmony your sight. At midnight, the sight you are giving to Harmony shall return to you. Do you agree to this, Medusa?"

Harmony: "No! I can't ask you to give me your sight, Medusa. Even for a night."

Medusa: "Harmony, you have too good a heart for your own good. I want to do this. Cyrene, I agree to hour terms. Please bestow my sight on Harmony for this night."

Cyrene grinned: "As you wish."

The room started to glow a soft blue. Soon the room fell away, like they were all floating in a giant ball of blue light. Lights like fireflies danced first around Medusa's head at her eye level. They danced around her head three times then performed the same around Harmony at Harmony's eye level. As the fireflies left Medusa, so did her sight. Her eyes were open but there was nothing but darkness. As the fireflies finished their dance around Harmony, Harmony's whole world changed. The world brightened. Harmony's eyes lit up seeing the world for the first time in her life. The light faded away, returning them to the interior of Medusa's cottage.

Harmony: "There's so much color!"

Medusa laughed: "It's quite the difference, isn't it?" She went to move toward Harmony and bumped into a table: "Owe! How did you not bump into everything? It's so dark and it's my house. I should be able to avoid things in my own living room."

Harmony: "I never knew anything different. You learn to navigate. Though I hope you don't have the time to adjust that well."

Medusa: "I'll rely on you to get around."

Harmony: "I will gladly be your eyes. Thank you for this gift."

Medusa: "You deserve it."

Harmony: "Oh but we were going to go to the Masquerade party."

Medusa: "We still are. I want you to see it. They go all out and if this is the one day you get to see, then I want you to get the most out of it."

Harmony: "Thank you. I...I don't know what to say."

Medusa: "Say you'll have fun and make the most of tonight. But I will definitely need your help to get around. I don't know how you lived like this so long. It's only been a few minutes and I'm already over the whole 'not seeing' thing."

Harmony: "I'll be happy to help you, though.....are you sure you're okay with this?"

Medusa: "Of course. You deserve it. And it only lasts till midnight, right? I can manage that long."

Harmony: "Thank you. This....I don't know how I'll ever be able to repay your kindness."

Medusa: "Your happiness is enough. Now, let's don our masks and get going."

Harmony: "Right! Shall I help you with yours?"

Medusa: "Please."

Harmony helps Medusa put on her mask: "So....how are we getting to the party?"

Cyrene: "Pegasus coach of course. They're really stunning creatures."

Harmony: "Pegasus coach? That's amazing! Tonight is going to feel like a dream."

Medusa: "Hopefully a beautiful dream that you won't soon forget."

Harmony: "It's one I will never forget. Thank you both for this gift. It's...it's just so amazing I don't have the words for it."

Cyrene: "Let's get going. The coach will be here soon. The party is hosted in a mansion on a cloud. It's really spectacular. But then, what would you expect from a party for the gods?"

Medusa: "They really do go all out. I...I've had some fun with it before. So long as they don't know it's me. Once they find out, they go back to their usual selves."

Cyrene: "Now you know that not everyone is horrible to you. Don't pretend like everyone hates you. It's not true."

Medusa: "It's not far from the truth, but I'm going to have fun this year, because Harmony is going to have the best night ever."

Cyrene: "I'll help where I can."

Medusa: "Thank you."

Cyrene led them outside. Medusa clung to Harmony to be her eyes. Harmony revelled in the sight. Two beautiful white horses with braided ribbons in their manes, and large beautiful wings that stretched 8 feet across. The carriage was open air so they would be able to see the city below as they flew. Harmony was practically dizzy with delight. Cyrene got in guided by the footman. She cleared her throat, waiting for Harmony and Medusa to follow.

Cyrene: "Are you two coming?"

Harmony: "Ah! Yes! Sorry! I was....they're stunning."

Medusa: "Everyone reacts that way at first. Wait till we're in the air and look down at the city."

Harmony: "I imagine it's stunning."

Medusa chuckles: "You won't have to imagine much longer."

Harmony: "True. Let's get you to the carriage."

Medusa: "I would appreciate that."

Harmony guided Medusa to the carriage and the footman helped each lady into the carriage. As they took to the air, the city fell away in a series of lit streets but on top of Acropolis Hill, the Parthenon was lit like a star. The Parthenon appeared to be an outline in a form of light. It took Harmony's breath away. As they climbed higher, a huge mansion appeared above the clouds. Key features mimicked those of Athens. Large columns were a key design to the mansion and there were several gardens. It was decorated in the theme of the hour. Lights flickered in the gardens in different themes. Some featured white crystals with light blue accents. One featured purple and orange. Still another was full of silver and gold. As they entered the large mansion, the columns towered over them, large enough for even the giant statue of Zeus to freely walk inside.

Cyrene: "Pretty, isn't it? You should feel lucky. Mortals aren't normally in attendance here."

Harmony: "It's....beautiful."

Medusa: "It's nothing compared to you."

Harmony blushed: "Th...Thank you."

Cyrene: "Well, what are we waiting for? Let's head in!"

Cyrene practically dragged them in. She was insistent on giving them a tour and talking about all the great architects that worked on the building and the techniques and design elements. Harmony happily listened and Medusa was content to follow along and hold onto Harmony. Harmony made sure to keep Medusa from getting hurt bumping into things. After a while, Medusa wanted to sneak Harmony away for a dance.

Harmony happily started to dance with Medusa. Even without Medusa's sight, she was an elegant lead with the waltz. Harmony stumbled some with the dancing but once Medusa took control, they were the stars of the room. The other dancers slowly stopped and circled the lovely couple to watch their movements.

They danced for hours, sometimes with others watching, and sometimes with other couples dancing around them. The world fell away and they were two stars shining and dancing as if the rest of the world didn't exist.

The world came back into focus though as someone approached and wanted to socialize. A girl in a turquoise gown and a deep blue mask over a pair of glasses approached. Her hair was a pretty shades of turquoise, light blue and sea green. It was kept down but it flowed as she walked: "Would you two care for a drink? You've been the bells of the ball."

Harmony gratefully accepted and thanked her for the drink. Medusa on the other hand turned cold: "I don't need anything from you. Why are you bothering us?"

The girl didn't seem to be affected by Medusa's comment. She seemed used to it: "You know I don't mean any ill will. You look lovely tonight Medusa. Enjoy some wine. It will help you relax. Bacchus made it himself."

Medusa: "I don't want any, Marina. Not from you or any of your family."

The girl sighed: "We've had this discussion before. I haven't done anything against you. Why do you hate me so much?"

Medusa: "I don't hate you. I hate your father. I can't see any of your family without thinking of him."

Marina: "I am not my father. I hope you can see that."

Medusa: "Actually, I can't see anything right now. So count yourself lucky."

Marina: "Why can't you see?"

Medusa: "None of your business.

Marina: "I'm not a bad person."

Medusa: "I know. I'm not saying you are. But you and the rest of your family just make me think of your father. I don't want to think of him and I don't want to see him."

Marina: "I'm not going to bring him here. You brought him up, not me. Also, I am not responsible for my father's actions."

Medusa: "I know you aren't. Let me just have some time to myself. Give me a few minutes. I don't want to ruin tonight for Harmony."

Harmony: "I don't want to leave you here alone."

Medusa: "I don't have anything against Marina. It's her father I can't stand. Go mingle for a few minutes and come back to get me. I should be calmer by then."

Harmony: "But..."

Medusa: "I'm fine. Go ahead. I'll be fine."

Marina: "We can go get her a drink. It will be fine and then you can check on her again."

Harmony: "Alright...I....I guess."

Marina led her to the drinks on the other side of the ballroom: "I hope you don't think poorly of the gods. Not all of them are as awful as Medusa makes them out to be."

Harmony: "She had a bad instance with one of the Gods. It's not unreasonable for her to be mad."

Marina: "I know she hates Poseidon and she has every right to, but people do change."

Harmony: "If he has changed, he should at least apologize to her. He caused her a lot of pain and grief."

Marina: "He did her wrong. I'm not disputing that. I just hope that you don't think that way about all of us."

Harmony: "I don't place his poor choices as a representation of all of the gods. I'm not familiar with your work though. What do you do?"

Marina: "I'm a marine biologist. Marina would be awful for a marine biologist so all of my actual human work is under the name Stephanie Shriver. I've studied the deepest seas and I'm still working on my research."

Harmony: "Oh, I've heard of your work. I never imagined you would be a Demigod."

Marina: "Oh, I understand. But it does afford me to explore the seas without issue."

Harmony: "How do you keep your glasses on underwater?"

Marina laughs: "I don't need them underwater. My sight issue is land based only. When I'm underwater, I don't have any difficulty seeing."

Harmony: "Really? That's pretty amazing."

Marina: "It's an adjustment on land but most of my time is spent in the oceans so it doesn't affect me that much. I'm actually a sea witch. I get to learn about the sea and write true stories about the creatures that live there. Sadly some of them are labeled as fantasy under a different name."

Harmony: "What do you mean?"

Marina: "Some humans are not ready to believe in mermaids or Gods or sirens or selkies."

Harmony: "You mean they're all real?"

Marina: "You're at a party hosted by two of the most well known gods and you are skeptical about mermaids, selkies, and sirens?"

Harmony laughs: "You have a good point."

Marina: "At any rate, I hope you don't think too badly of us. Just because we're Gods, Goddesses, and demigods, doesn't mean we're all as terrible as Poseidon was to Medusa. What he did to her was wrong and everyone who knows the truth, know how awful he was. He gets pretty jealous and I like to think he has learned from his mistakes."

Harmony: "I don't think everyone here is like that, but Poseidon really hurt her. I don't think he ever even apologized to her."

Marina: "If you can convince him to apologize to her, I would be impressed. I will warn you though, he does not think highly of mortals. Most of the gods don't. It's no offense to you, but it's just how they are and they are stuck in their ways."

Harmony: "Poseidon isn't going to be here, is he?"

Marina: "Oh, no, I knew Medusa would probably be here so I made sure to keep him busy tonight."

Harmony: "How did you manage that?"

Marina: "I made sure to stir up a little trouble for him. It will keep him busy all night."

Harmony: "That's not very nice."

Marina: "It was the only way to guarantee he wouldn't come. If he came, it would chase Medusa off. You saw how upset she was that I was here. Imagine if dad was."

Harmony sighed: "You have a point."

Marina: "I should let you get back to Medusa. Enjoy the rest of the party. By the way, I recommend spending some time in the south garden while you're here. It's beautiful and the air is crisp and fresh."

Harmony: "Oh, ah, thank you."

Harmony returned to Medusa, wandering through the crowd.
Harmony: "Feeling better?"

Medusa let out a large sigh: "Better. I'm sorry about that. I...I'm still not over it."

Harmony: "No, it's okay. Really. I can't imagine what you are even going through."

Medusa: "Believe me, you never want to find out. Shall we dance?"

Harmony: "Sure. Let's."

Harmony helped Medusa up and slowly led he to the dance floor. Harmony took the lead and they danced for hours, lost in their own little world. When they danced, it felt like the world fell away and it was just the two of them, dancing on clouds. They danced right out to the south garden. The garden glittered and the breeze was soft and pleasant. Near midnight, a countdown began. As the count began, the two slowed their dance and leaned close. 5...4....3.... The two were so close they could feel each other's breath. 2...1... The moment the countdown ceased, it felt like the world stood still as their lips met. One simple, gentle kiss sent the world spinning. Light swirled around them both. They floated above the ground. Harmony's hair floated up like she was floating in water. Medusa's snakes that she had grown so accustomed to had become beautiful long flowing hair. Harmony opened her eyes from the kiss to find she could no longer see but she felt out of breath. Still stunned from their kiss. Medusa too felt breathless. They stood there for a few minutes in silence.

After a couple minutes of silence, Medusa finally spoke: "You're beautiful."

Harmony blushed deeply: "Ah, thank you. You are beautiful too. That was...that was...I think I love you."

Medusa: "L...love?" She stammered. She was startled.

Harmony: "Yes. I love you."

Medusa: "Snakes, scary eyes and all?"

Harmony laughed: "Snakes, scary eyes, and all. Including anything else you want to include. I love you. Medusa, finding you was the best thing that ever happened to me."

Medusa: "I...I don't know what to say. No one has ever accepted me as a monster."

Harmony: "You aren't a monster. You are a beautiful, shining star that people have been too blind to see."

Medusa kissed Harmony again. Their kiss deepened and then as Harmony felt where Medusa's snakes had been was soft and silky hair, she gave a startled squeak. Medusa pulled back frowning.

Medusa: "What's wrong?"

Harmony: "Your snakes! They're gone! I...I don't feel them!"

Medusa was startled: "What?!" Medusa felt Her now soft hair. "I...my curse...I....I think I'm cured!"

Harmony: "You...you mean the curse is...?"

Medusa: "It's gone! I'm mortal again!"

Medusa was so thrilled she was practically jumping up and down. She grabbed Harmony's hands and spun around: "I'm free!"

A stunning woman came out into the garden. An owl at her shoulder. "What is all this excitement?"

Medusa shut up instantly and eyed the woman.

Harmony: "We were ah, celebrating."

The woman smiled: "Oh? And what were you celebrating?"

Medusa: "The....the end to the curse you placed on me. My eyes stopped turning people to stone and now my snakes are gone. I'm mortal again, right?"

The woman's smile grew: "Indeed Medusa. True love will break a curse. You have found true love it seems."

Medusa: "Is this the end then? I'm free...forever?"

The woman frowned: "Not exactly. True love freed you from your curse. If you stray from your love, or if you are unfaithful, or if you forsake your love, the curse will return and if that happens, it will not be removed."

Medusa: "I don't think that will be an issue."

Harmony: "You cursed her in the first place unjustly! You never should have cursed her to begin with!"

Medusa: "Harmony! Please apologize to Lady Athena! She can and will punish you!"

Harmony: "You haven't had anyone stand up for you. If I had been there, I would have done this back when she cursed you!"

Athena looked amused more than angry: "Harmony, you are correct, she did not deserve to be cursed, but there are things you need to understand."

Medusa and Harmony were both struck silent. They couldn't believe that Athena would agree with them or admit it.

Athena: "Ladies, have a seat."

They both sit and wait for her to continue. Athena looks them over and then has a seat herself.

Athena: "There are a few reasons for what I did. But let me tell you what I saw and what I considered. The day Medusa was coming to my temple, Poseidon and I had gotten into a small argument. He was still upset with me for winning the city of Athens. The people of Athens still valued Poseidon because the city was very much still part of the sea. His temple was the last thing they saw when they left by sea. He saw you heading toward my temple. He thought at first that he could lure you away from me and that you would convert others. You were so proud of your beauty and did not see him for who he was, so in his anger, he sought to punish you. He followed you into my temple and tore your purity from you. Mortals can be quite cruel. There would have been only one position you could have then, and that would be a harlot. A street walker. A mistress. I was very angry that there would be such an incident in my temple. I couldn't retaliate against Poseidon. He is my uncle and to go against him would have caused a rift. He also would have targeted you again to defile you again. I took these things into consideration and applied to you a curse. I turned you into a Gorgon. The snakes would provide protection and a visual deterrent. Your ability to change others to stone would apply as a form of protection. It would serve as protection against my uncle if nothing else. Besides, you two never would have met if I didn't extend your lifetime."

Medusa sat in silent contemplation for a moment: "I....I don't know what to say...."

Athena: "I know it's a lot. Why don't you two head home and get some rest? If you want to talk to me later, come to the temple of Athena and I will be waiting."

Harmony: "Thank you for your story."

Athena: "You are welcome. Be safe and get some rest."

Harmony and Medusa headed back and crashed on the couch. Their minds still whirling from everything that happened that night. Their relationship, and the revelation from Athena.

Chapter 7: Changes

The next morning, breakfast was quiet. Neither Medusa nor Harmony knew how to address the occurrences of the night before. So much had happened that they didn't know where to begin. That's when times where friends come over are extremely helpful.

Cyrene popped into the kitchen and slung an arm around Medusa: "what's shakin bacon?"

Medusa glared: "Get off me. I'm cooking. Plus I don't think that's an appropriate use of that phrase."

Cyrene let go of her smiling: "who cares if it's the right version? It's my version and it's appropriate since you're actually making bacon."

Medusa: "I'm making breakfast and you were not invited."

Cyrene: "Awe, come on. I'm totally your favorite person. Well, I mean besides your girlfriend."

Harmony and Medusa's faces lit up bright red.

Cyrene: "Awe, how cute! You two are being all shy and stuff."

Harmony: "We ah...well you see..."

Medusa: "We kissed, I liked it, she broke my curse, we haven't talked about it, it's none of your business."

Cyrene laughed: "Oh my. Well you two have a lot to talk about. So when do you get to meet her parents?"

Medusa pales: "Meet her p...parents?"

Cyrene: "Yeah, you know, you're supposed to meet the parents before you can ask for her hand in marriage."

Medusa: "We hadn't gotten anywhere near that kind of...! I mean...we...Ah...I....Harmony, help."

Harmony: "Um, can we change the subject? I think there's a lot Medusa and I need to discuss in private."

Cyrene: "But it's an interesting conversation and you two have been like playing the quiet game or something. Oh, and Marina wants to chat with you two at some point."

Medusa: "I want nothing to do with any of Poseidon's kids. He's done enough damage in my life."

Cyrene: "Good things can come out of bad situations too you know. I mean, you wouldn't even know Harmony if you hadn't been cursed."

Medusa: "Whose side are you on?! Poseidon forced me. I could have ended up the mother of one of his kids!"

Cyrene: "But you aren't.... But you're dating Harmony."

Medusa: "What does that have to do with anything?"

Cyrene: "Ah ha! So you admit it!"

Medusa: "Cyrene!"

Cyrene: "Relax. I'm only teasing you. You need to relax. It's fine."

Harmony: "She's stressed enough. Your teasing isn't helping. She needs to figure out where she goes from here. Her curse is broken. She can do whatever she wants. Go where she wants, be who she wants."

Medusa: "Um, thanks. Honestly, I....I really do want to be with you. I ah....I think I..."

Harmony: "I love you too."

Cyrene: "You two are like elementary school kids. Just kiss already."

Medusa: "We don't need an audience."

Cyrene: "Yeah, Yeah. Well, Marina wants to meet. At least let Harmony meet with her. It's important to Marina and junk. So stop being an anemone and stinging everyone that comes near. Let her go meet and don't give her grief about it. Marina wants to talk and it's incredibly important to Marina."

Medusa: "Fine! If it will get you to shut up!"

Cyrene: "Oh thanks. That was easier than I thought."

Medusa: "She will have 30 minutes to say what she needs to say and then we are leaving."

Cyrene: "You're actually going to meet with her too?"

Medusa: "Of course. I don't trust Poseidon not to get involved and possibly hurt Harmony."

Cyrene: "Awe. That's so cute."

Medusa: "I'm realistic, not cute."

Harmony: "You are perfect as you are."

Medusa blushed: "So are you."

Harmony: "When is the meeting?"

Cyrene: "She's out of town till the 17th for a conference but she can meet with you that night. Say, 6ish?"

Harmony: "Okay. We will be there."

Cyrene: "Great! Now what's for breakfast?"

Medusa: "None for you. Now go bother someone else. You weren't invited."

Cyrene: "Awe, Alright. Lovebird breakfast it is. But I'm stealing some bacon." She grabbed a piece from the pan, stuck it in her mouth and disappeared.

Harmony: "Well, that was eventful."

Medusa: "More than I like. Breakfast is ready."

Harmony: "Oh, thank you."

Medusa dishes up their plates and then sat down with her to eat.

Harmony: "Ah, you know, I've been thinking...I would love it if you moved in with me. I mean, you don't have to but I..."

Medusa: "I'd love to live with you. But how about we use my place instead? It's more private. No prying eyes. Well, besides Cyrene but there's no getting around that."

Harmony: "She's just trying to be a good friend."

Medusa: "Yeah, I know, but sometimes I just don't want it. She has too much sunshine and rainbows sometimes."

Harmony: "She cares about your happiness. So do I."

Medusa: "Well, we have a couple weeks before we need to meet up with Marina, so let's make the most of it. I have all sorts of places we can go and things we can do."

Harmony smiled: "What are we waiting for? Let's make the most of the day."

Medusa smiled: alright, let's get to it."

The next couple of weeks were like a dream. They were free to get out and have coffee and go to events and Medusa didn't need to hide. She was free to bask in the sunshine and be flirty with Harmony.

The day they were to meet with Marina, Medusa was extremely stressed and kept trying to talk Harmony out of them going. Any reason they shouldn't or couldn't go was enough for Medusa. Harmony would remind Medusa that she had agreed to meet with Marina and Medusa would try to think of some other objection. In the end, they both went to meet Marina. They got a private room at a nice restaurant and waited for Marina to arrive. Marina stumbled into the room. She was clearly very nervous.

Marina: "Ah, so, thank you both for coming."

Medusa: "Just when I thought I was free of you immortals, you called this meeting. What is it you want?"

Marina: "Well, I have something important to tell Harmony and I didn't want it to come as any more of a surprise to you as to her."

Medusa: "What are you talking about?"

Marina: "Harmony hasn't talked about her dad, has she?"

Harmony: "I know nothing about my father except that he's from around here. Mom met him on a vacation."

Medusa: "What does that have to do with you, Marina?"

Marina: "I know her dad. So do you."

Harmony: "You do? Really?"

Medusa: "You'd better not be suggesting what I think you're suggesting."

Marina: "Harmony and I are half sisters. Poseidon is both our fathers. I've been watching over Harmony since she was born and hiding her existence from our father."

Medusa: "No! You're lying!"

Marina: "I'm not lying. It's true. She has the birthmark on her left shoulder. Same as mine."

Harmony: "You have the same birthmark? Is...is it really true?"

Medusa: "You've been planning this, haven't you?! This whole time, I thought...! Well, I won't be the fool any more! I'm free of the curse and I don't want anything to do with either of you ever again!"

Medusa ran crying angry tears. Harmony tried to plead with her to wait and tried to pursue her but Marina held her there.

Marina: "She needs time. So do you. I was hoping that telling you both at the same time would prevent this but...I'm sorry. I know how much you love her."

Harmony: "We were planning to move in together."

Marina hugged Harmony: "I'm so sorry. But it's better to come out now than later."

Harmony: "I'm afraid of losing her."

Marina: "You two are meant to be. You'll be together again. It may just take a few centuries."

Harmony: "Centuries?!"

Marina: "Or less....hopefully...."

Harmony: "It's not that I'm not appreciative of knowing who I am, or rather where I come from but, Poseidon was a real jerk! He hurt Medusa and instead of being punished, his transgression is ignored! It's wrong!"

Marina: "I'm not arguing that. He did wrong and some day he may have to answer for it, but right now, you are very worked up and I think you need rest. I have a place here. You can stay with me for a few days. Maybe it will help you relax and give Medusa some space."

Harmony: "I....thank you."

Harmony settled with Marina and talked for a while. They eventually went to Marina's house and Marina set Harmony up with a bed. Harmony spent the following couple days mostly in bed upset.

Marina finally got her to come out after a few days: "Harmony, have faith. She can't be mad forever..."

Harmony put her head in her arms on the table: "She has held a grudge against Poseidon for centuries."

Marina: "Yes but....She will come around eventually. I mean, what dad did isn't your fault and you didn't even know who your dad was initially. I tried to tell you with her there so she would know you didn't know but...well...she um, she doesn't trust easily and it backfired. I'm so sorry, Harmony."

Harmony raised her head a bit: "I miss her. Will you help me find her and bring her home? I had to get help from Cyrene in order to find her the last time she ran away."

Marina: "Cyrene knew that we were sisters. She has better sight on land than I do. She knew who you were before you two met. But I'm sure she will help and I will do everything I can to help you. We are family after all."

Harmony: "I don't know whether to be happy or sad right now. But I appreciate the help."

Marina: "I will always be here for you."

Harmony put her head back down and stayed that way for a while longer. After a few more days, Marina was able to start getting Harmony to get out of the house and start searching for Medusa together. They spent a few weeks looking before Marina broached the subject of actually meeting Poseidon.

Harmony: "I would love to meet him and give him a piece of my mind. He needs to apologize to Medusa at the absolute very least."

Marina: "Um...I will introduce you and let you figure that out."

Harmony nodded: "I will figure that out. Please introduce me."

Marina: "Ah, gladly."

Marina arranged the meeting for a few days later at the temple of Poseidon. She made sure the temple would be off limits with the general belief that it was closed for restoration. She helped Harmony dress up, though Harmony didn't really want to.

Marina: "May I introduce to you, Poseidon, God of the sea. Poseidon, father, may I introduce to you, my little sister and your youngest daughter, Harmony."

Harmony had a deep frown set on her lips: "I can't see you."

Poseidon, surprised, came closer from 10 feet away, to 5 feet away. "Can you see me now?"

Harmony: "No."

He again moved closer, now 2 feet away: "How about now?"

Harmony: "No."

He moved in close to where he was leaning in close and wondering why she had such poor eyesight: "Surely you can see me now?"

SMACK!

Harmony's hand collided soundly with Poseidon's cheek. He held his cheek in shock as Harmony continued her response: "No. I am blind. I couldn't see you if I wanted to. I don't want to see you. I want you to understand that what you did to Medusa was wrong and that you owe her at the very minimum a heartfelt apology. Until you do that, I want nothing to do with you. I love Medusa. Your deeds resulted in her curse and just when we broke her curse so she could be free, Marina said I was your daughter. Medusa thinks I betrayed her. She thinks I lied to her. This mess is your fault and I want you to help fix it. Find Medusa and apologize properly. While you are at it, you can apologize to Athena for using Medusa in Athena's temple. If Medusa never has anything to do with me again, I will make sure you never forget it and always regret it. Do you understand?"

Poseidon stared at her a long moment: "I'll give you this, you have guts. That's for sure. Why should I apologize to her?"

Harmony: "You should apologize because you were the one in the wrong. I love Medusa. She thinks I betrayed her because you happen to be my father. If you want to be part of my life and start over, you will apologize to Medusa and be sincere. I am not afraid of you. As your child or not, I am my own woman and I will fight for my love."

Marina: "Dad, she's serious. She's been crying since Medusa ran off. Would it really hurt your pride that much to apologize rather than facing the anger of your children?"

Poseidon: "Children?"

Marina: "I'm siding with Harmony on this. I will stop helping you with the sea and I will cause trouble for you like I did the night of the masquerade. You'll be so busy chasing sea creatures and putting your realm back in order that you won't be able to sleep, let alone do anything else."

Poseidon cringed: "You wouldn't dare."

Harmony: "Try us."

Poseidon: "Fine, you win. I'll apologize. But I'm only doing this once."

Marina: "Apologize to Athena too."

Poseidon glared: "And why should I?"

Harmony: "Because you wronged them both. Your apology is long overdue."

Marina: "You're righting one wrong. You may as well right both of your wrongs. Do the right thing for once. Be a father we can be proud of."

Poseidon: "I'm going to regret this."

Harmony: "You should never regret doing the right thing." Her expression softened: "Be the father we can be proud of so we can build a relationship based on truth and honesty."

Poseidon: "I'm a god. That should be enough to make you proud."

Harmony: "Doing the right thing will make us proud. Being a God is no different from being a mortal to me. Everyone is equal and deserves equal respect. Please find Medusa and bring her home."

Poseidon: "I will do my best for you. I don't understand your affection for Medusa but if it means this much to both of you...well, I'll try. I will see you again soon. I hope to be better received when I do."

Harmony: "If you have done the right thing, I will be waiting with open arms."

Poseidon: "Alright." He disappeared into the sea.

Marina: "Harmony, that took some real guts. Medusa will be sad to have missed that. It will make one hell of a story later though."

Harmony: "It's not about the story. I probably shouldn't have slapped him, but I don't think he would have understood the pain he caused otherwise."

Marina: "He will find her and you'll be happy again. Just be patient and I will support you in the meantime."

Harmony hugged her sister: "Thank you."

Marina: "Any time. Let's go home."

Harmony nodded and they walked back to Marina's place in close silence.

Chapter 8: Christmas

On December 24th, Poseidon returned, this time showing up to Marina's house in the middle of the night with a figure thrown over his shoulder kicking and making muffled sounds. He set down the figure that was tied up and gagged.

Marina and Harmony got up startled from their Christmas movie by his sudden arrival.

Poseidon: "As I said, I'm only doing this once. Therefore, Medusa, sit down and listen closely."

He set her on the couch and cleared his throat as Medusa glared daggers at him. Her snakes had returned and hissed their displeasure.

Poseidon: "Medusa, my girls stood up for you and insisted that I do the right thing and apologize to you for the distress I put you in. I'm not good at apologies so you'll have to forgive my presentation. I brought you here so that Harmony could hear this and because she told me she loves you. I'm a God. I did things in my youth that I am not proud of. I hurt you to get back at Athena. I am sorry for what I have done and the suffering you experienced because of it. I ask that you don't blame the innocent for what I did. Harmony loves you and you shouldn't take your anger at me out on her. Please forgive me."

Medusa stared at him in shock. Marina removed Medusa's bindings and gag while she was calm. Medusa didn't say anything for a very long time. She finally spoke in a quiet voice: "I never thought I would hear those words from you. I don't think I can ever forgive you for what you did.....but, I think I can learn to stop hating you. Before I knew Harmony was your daughter, I...I learned to love. When your name came up, I felt my world crashing down. I....I got scared and my snakes came back. My curse is back and it's probably never going away again."

Harmony: "I never minded your snakes. They are one thing that makes you special. I love you as you are; as you have always been." She got down on one knee: "I may not have a ring and I don't know whether we can be together officially, but I love you and I want you to always be a part of my life. Will you be my whole world and promise to stay with me forever?"

Medusa: "You want to marry me? Me? Medusa, the horrible gorgon?"

Harmony: "No, I want to marry you, Medusa, the wonderful person I fell in love with that accepted a blind woman without question."

Medusa and Harmony kissed. A year later....they were wed. Poseidon himself presided over the wedding.

The end.

Table of Content

References

"Athena, the Greek Goddess of War and Wisdom." *The Creation Myth According to Ancient Greeks*. Web. 10 Dec. 2018.

"Book Your Ferry to Poros Island." *Greeka*. Web. 10 Dec. 2018.

"Kerry Kolasa-Sikiaridi." *News from Greece*. Greece.GreekReporter.com Latest News from Greece, 11 June 2017. Web. 10 Dec. 2018.

"Odeon of Herodes Atticus: History, Pictures and Useful Information." *Vision - Past & Present*. 22 Dec. 2016. Web. 10 Dec. 2018.

"Piraeus." *Google Search*. Google. Web. 10 Dec. 2018

"Sounio Poseidon Temple in Athens." *Greeka*. Web. 10 Dec. 2018.

"The Olympians." *Greek Mythology Gods Olympians*. Web. 10 Dec. 2018.

"The Timeless Myth of Medusa, a Rape Victim Turned Into a Monster." *Google Search*. Google. Web. 10 Dec. 2018.

Experience, To Do and, To Stay Eat & Play, To Get Around & Be a Smarter Traveller, What's On in Athens Now, and People Trends Culture. "Athens Events - What's on in Athens Greece." *Why Athens*. Web. 10 Dec. 2018.

Experience, To Do and, To Stay Eat & Play, To Get Around & Be a Smarter Traveller, What's On in Athens Now, and People Trends Culture. "Odeon of Herodes Atticus - Detailed Guide and Events | Why Athens City Guide." *Why Athens*. 28 May 2018. Web. 10 Dec. 2018.

www.ingramcontent.com/pod-product-compliance
Lightning Source LLC
Chambersburg PA
CBHW020514160726
47991CB00007B/2950